Cold Ashes

A Tabloid of Emotions

Cold Ashes
Edited & compiled by
Anirban Dutta

Paperback Edition

First published in India in 2024 by

Inkfeathers Publishing
Vivek Vihar, New Delhi 110095
www.inkfeathers.com

ISBN 978-81-19483-42-6

Cold Ashes

A Tabloid of Emotions

Edited & compiled by

Anirban Dutta

Inkfeathers Publishing
www.inkfeathers.com

Disclaimer

The anthology "Cold Ashes" is a collection of 6 short stories and 33 poems written by 23 authors who belong to different parts of the world.

Unless otherwise indicated, all the names, characters, objects, businesses, places, events, incidents—whether physical/non-physical, real/unreal, tangible/ intangible in whatsoever description used in this book are either the product of the author's imagination or used in a fictitious manner. Any resemblance to actual persons, objects, entities, living or dead, or actual events is purely coincidental.

The contents published in this book are solely owned by their respective authors and are in no way intended to hurt anyone's religious, political, spiritual, brand, personal or fanatic beliefs and/or faith, whatsoever. In case, any sort of plagiarism is detected in the contents within this anthology or in case of any complaints, grievances, or objections, neither the anthology editor nor the publisher is to be held responsible.

Dedicated to all the authors.

Featuring the contributions of

Callum Wilson, Aryan Malkani, Charvi Mishra,

Lokeshna Bulan, Simi Tiwari, Tulsi Nambiar, Anirban Dutta,

Mahek Gupta, Sakhi Singh, P. Navya, Samriddhi Khawas,

Pranjal Verma, Bhakti Barad, Nainika Chaudhari,

Tarini Bhatia, Ankur Mondal, Keertika Shivee,

Malavika Sahoo, Shari Gharat, Saisha Khemka,

Shrishti Tibdewal, Kanak Modi, Shravani Kapoor

Contents

Meet the Editor

Anirban Dutta

Anirban Dutta is a Research Associate at the Strategic Studies Centre of The Geostrata. He also acted as the Tactical Intelligence Analyst at Max Security Solutions Ltd., Mumbai. Upon completing his post-graduate degree in International Studies from the Symbiosis International (Deemed University), Pune, he has contributed to various anthologies and has published a travel anthology titled "In A Voyager's Shoes." He has also been featured at The New Indian Express, Daily Hunt and News 24 India for his literary contributions.

Editor's Note

From life's challenges to unending emotional gaps, the anthology allows you to uncover and nurture the unknown ashes of your life. This made a curious author explore the idea of an anthology that reveals the depth of emotions and thoughts touching the lives of countless individuals. The concept of anthology had its beginning on a sunny but windy day. The sunny day turned out cloudy as clouds with the colour of coal approached the unknown horizon. A time when the fields of grain dance with the hustling sound of the wind soon to turn itself into a gathering storm.

Days passed, and the heavy rains gave way to editing and compiling short stories and poems. The anthology made sound attempts to unite the stories and poems of authors. The idea is to connect and uncover the hidden emotions of diverse individuals in the form of a book. The book gives a voice to the unheard, unburnished feelings. The different chapters in the anthology are to question the hidden taboo of expressing one's feelings openly. The anthology aims to include the concept of individual emotions into the book's primary genre.

The book has significantly departed from the established notions of feelings associated with untimely incidents like death.

In this anthology, sound attempts have been made to unite the two themes dealing with untimely incidents and feelings.

The anthology has attempted to twist and turn to express untouched feelings with the creativity of the short story and the beauty of a poem. The anthology has tried to bring in the emotions and reactions closely associated with sadness and unravel the feelings related to anxiousness, depression, crisis, doubt, worries and sorrow.

The book of emotions attempts to make readers realise that the outer expression and outburst of sadness cannot always be linked with unconscious feelings of desperation. The anthology allows the reader to unite various emotions under separate themes into a book. The collection deals with incidents closely aligned with real-life experiences, making them go through short stories and poems.

The anthology is an idea that has stood the ups and downs of time and emotions, making the anthology a remarkable cocktail of sadness and beauty that transforms itself as sweet upon reading.

So, read the anthology that has survived the taste of emotions and time expressed by a few remarkable individuals.

POEMS

HEAD PIPES

Callum Wilson

I think I like it when I'm alone.

It makes me feel like I'm home.

There is a poison that sometimes leaks out of the pipes in my head.

Acrid, sweaty sewage air that dribbles out my brain.

Some of it is strawberry-sweet, blinkingly tart, and sweetly repulsive.

It places me beside the sea of pink, crimson troubles,

And swirling bubbles that keep my island bobbing on.

I don't know why it is that colour,

But I now know not to bother,

Learning things that crowd and smother,

And the silence cradles me in a thunderous aporia.

The glory of an endless rain that doesn't stop for stories of the times when time mattered less than it does now today.

The silence isn't as gentle as it once seemed,
And it starts to scream and cry, but that is good.
I'll tell you why it isn't good to keep things all inside,
Because you could die,
Let the billows swallow you.
The end will come when you are due.
Don't worry about the little things like fear, dear.
Today, I sat there in my yellow room where the wallpaper doesn't talk,
At my wonky bureau that needs a new haze of varnish,
And I stared out of the boarded-up windows,
Shoddy planks badly obscure a faded, wilting grassland.
An amble of a chartreuse zephyr, patiently swaying.
A spine of endless gas pipework had torn through it all,
From my room to the rest of everything, it was monotone,
I think I like it when I'm alone.
It makes me feel like I'm home.
There is a potent consternation that coils.
It is in a throbbing vein and boils you,
It breathes heady, chunky sewage gas,
That leaks outside and makes me thrash,
And makes my eyes go purple.

All the words inside spray out in vapours.

The words are an acrid rancour against your silence.

They don't pamper your pretty-tart-violence.

A diatribe in fog leaves me through the top.

My head is your masterpiece,

A picturesque pipework dug into my skull.

I am your virgin white clover.

My umbels of grimy iron breed.

Noxious toxins that wither my roots.

I think I like being alone.

It makes me feel at home.

That monotone world has split apart into a shower of hallowed, vibrant dew.

The dandelion walls keep me safe,

The verdant land floats through the decaying ice seas.

Although the silence isn't as gentle as it once seemed to me,

My diadem of leaky pipes, strung together by fraying wire,

Breathes in its' inescapable sleeping fog.

ALETHIOLOGY

Mahek Gupta

I am reminded of being human once,
Sense of smell assaults me, with no escape.
Petrichor running down my naked muons,
Displaced to the past, jagged edges scrape.

We hide in each other. Our breaths mesh. Eyes shut.
Thunder blankets us, frames what we're built with,
Photons traverse our instincts, warning gut,
Shivers crash us; foul warmth taints our old myth.

In present times, the sky calls for time toll,
The smooth ledge calms my taut muscles and mind.
Fast wind. Slow fall. Broken bones. Happy soul. Fall.
Earth pulls me to my only path. We're bound.

Blood still coddles cobblestones. Body is long gone.
My waif swims, searching for the hell it spawns.

THE NOMAD

Shrishti Tibdewal

I don't know how to write,
Expression and acceptance have never,
Exactly been a strong suit of mine.
There are days I feel like a nomad,
For the others, I call myself a writer.
I had a dream once,
I was absent,
Darkness and nothingness succumbed to me.
I suddenly began falling,
Attempting to hold onto something,
Scared and unable to move,
Waiting to feel the thunder against me,
And fall into pieces the way,
I imagined someday I would be on the moon.

Then I let go, I surrendered,

Waiting for the fall,

But it never came.

I discerned I wasn't falling.

It was an ocean,

I was drowning.

It felt peaceful,

To let go and let it consume me.

The darkness was now tempting,

The nomad found his home,

I never knew how to write,

Yet, I ended up inscribing on a stone.

CHANGE

Kanak Modi

I guess chalk powder and cocaine aren't that
different after all.

Nothing's changed.

Turns out red paint and blood look are quite similar in
themselves.

Nothing's changed.

Dead and Dad are the same thing until they aren't.

The extra 'e' stands for epiphanies that distort my reality.

Nothing's changed.

Everything's changed.

The internet says change replaces things for the better.

My mother ties my hands to the doorknob and screams,

Clipping skin and paper.

I mumble, saying I thought staplers were used to
hold things together.

She bursts into tears and throws herself in my chest.
Everything's changed.
My therapist is a man my dad's age.
You'd say that turns around the narrative,
Someone the same kind, newer, and better.
But nothing's changed.
My body's fixated on old things.
I'm used to stale coffee.
Fresh cappuccino burns my tongue and ruins all taste.
Is this a change?
God, life hasn't changed.
There's nothing new and better about this rage.
I'm sorry.
This poem was supposed to be about change.
Ghosts sleep in bed with me and say I've changed.
I scare them, and they get furious.
Then, they leave.
My pillow is seven years old, and it hasn't changed.
Nothing's changed.
Nothing has to change.

PERFECT

Shravani Kapoor

When you believe that things are finally perfect,

Life throws at you a new conquest.

To acquire this, you are required to start a new chapter.

A chapter you really didn't see coming,

One you never really anticipated or ever thought of.

You may not be able to plan this chapter,

With a definite attitude, but you can start with,

A single letter, then a word, a phrase, then a sentence,

As you keep writing it, you will again become comfortable and stubborn,

Towards ending this chapter and starting a new one,

But whenever you get used to something,

And resist ending or changing it,

You will expect another door that you will inevitably enter,

Not because you wanted to,

But just because life wants you to never settle and
wants you to challenge yourself.

This door doesn't open when you want it to,
and that's because you still,

Have things to do and complete in this chapter,

But neither will this door open with a warning.

Instead, it opens when you are cemented towards your
comfort and don't want to let go.

So, even if we believe we are ready for change,
whenever change,

Approaches us, we might not be ready for it,

But that change is certainly prepared for us.

DWINDLING

Ankur Mondal

When I looked through the window,
I saw you.
I saw you wrecked.
I gazed through your cracks.
I saw you damaged.
The sublime rays falling on your body,
Made your dwindling evident.
And then, in retrospect,
I saw myself.
Yes, you reflected on me,
My soul.
Yet, we are both here,
Standing tall,
Sturdy.
The melancholy of our tribulation,
Always attested to the attention of onlookers.

LUCENT GRIEF

Mahek Gupta

I have some pain in scattered parts of three
At times like this.
Times when I need peace
I can placate it to pinpricks in me
My flesh needs us.
I beg, 'Cosmos, hold me?'

The pinpricks tune to the beat of the stars.
Thoughts scrape the rusty floor to blindly follow.
Broken constellations in me, they hiss.
Treat us like tumours. Forevermore bleed.

I grasp each piece. One by one, they come home.
I was grinning when the first stars collide.
Burn. Smelt. Forge. I smirk. Cosmos renounces me.
I fail to escape this infernal life.

Focused on the pain of the stars, I feel peace.
Exiled, lost, forgotten in the swan song, I merge.

FUNNY LITTLE THING CALLED ANXIETY

Bhakti Barad

The funny little thing, that is, anxiety comes and goes,

Like a pandemic full of pity.

You'll find it in streets with car trunks full of frozen embarrassment in a malice city.

Look under your sheets, under your feet.

A rotten piece of meat,

Something you can't beat there.

You will meet this funny little thing called anxiety,

With blue lips and a few flips,

Having tea with your insecurity.

Look under the rug of the future,

There it sits,

Wearing a cloak of invisibility.

It is still testing the horses in our heads,

Bidding on the way,

We'll sweat.

It doesn't spill our secrets,

It is our secret,

A barrel rolling down the last thread,

It comes with a company and a silent disco of panic attacks.

Drinks from the hot and cold punch bowls drip down
our backs,

Bangs on the doors of your pulse in fear,

You run in your converse,

You run faster,

But it always comes first with a touch of popularity
in this distressed city.

There lives a funny little thing called anxiety.

DARK MINDS

Shravani Kapoor

Agony has swallowed every inch of my existence.
Numbness has engulfed me into a sadist.
Sleepiness is soon going to encompass me with nocturnal,
Before, I became one myself.
The pain, still indescribable,
Remains deep-seated within me,
Yet, I choose for it to stay stubborn.

HOUSE TURNED CEMETERY

Kanak Modi

Snow falls off from the pine trees.
Stuck but racing down uncontrollably.
I adore the beautiful sight of snow,
Except for a fall, they slap your skin,
And numb you till your bones,
Grow hard and freeze.
A sudden cold stiffens and floats in the air,
As water turns to stone.
Cuts in dresses, age like fine wine,
But ageing in my flesh dreads the mind.
It assumes ridges and creases,
The wires in my body.
An overheated filament,
A flickering bulb,
Smashed to the marble floor.

Pretence smiles,
Cherry lips, austere fronts, indifference,
Accompanies the venom that his silence,
Diffuses within my ardent soul.
A morgue inside a house,
A home-turned graveyard,
It shelters a breathing corpse.
My heart is already a cemetery.
Disregard but stained rugs, broken crockery,
Torn blinds, sombre sheet,
Often wreaks a defeatist's heart,
Hours pass again,
I am awake but frozen.

GROWING UP

Sakhi Singh

Growing up is a lot like cutting a mango.

You try to peel off the skin and eventually call your
father to help.

You do it perfectly.

Your house is a soft summer of laughter until
there is no sun left for you to feel,

But there is always a trace of light on the floor,
even when the night falls.

You're twenty-one now, and you remember how your mother
made mango shakes for you when you were young,

You ask her if she could make some for you tomorrow,

And maybe every day if she has the time.

You hope she does.

You do not want to forget the brief moments,

When you didn't feel like you were carrying a shadow
of everything,

You shouldn't have done.

When you didn't try to spit out bits of everything,

That made you because someone once told you that you were too loud,

And that taking less space like a dainty flower could improve your chances of being 'liked.'

So, you looked at yourself in the mirror at fifteen,

Poked at the fat on your stomach and thighs with a scissor,

If only there were a small doll in place of you.

Is there no market for, well… making exchanges?

You try to cut the mango into perfect squares,

Sucking the juice off of your thumb every now and then.

It's of no use, you tell yourself and laugh.

Your mango isn't nearly perfect enough,

It's not even close.

Your hands are sticky, and you don't want to have it anymore,

But you're also too hungry to care.

It's a little like planning your years on glossy paper and pouring even more glitter on it,

Eventually realising that it's not real anymore.

So, you stick to regular paper.

Sometimes, you might tear it,

You might fold it into halves and quarters,

But it's still yours snug inside your pocket,

And you know you're going to buy a whole stack of glossy paper,

Why does everything have to be real only when you close your eyes?

You're done cutting the mango,

You sit on the stool and begin to eat it.

It's four o'clock, and the sun is a soft glow of a sleeping afternoon,

Your best friend once lived next door to you,

Now, there are only numbers between the two of you,

You hope to cut a mango for her someday.

A friend had once shown you how snowflakes settled on his sleeve,

You wish to show him the light on your feet.

The boy you love–in a different city–loves eating mangoes.

You hope he is eating them too, probably at the same time as you.

You plan to send him a sunflower tomorrow.

You feel your mother's fingers on your shoulder,

'I'll make mango shake for you,' she says,

And you hold her hand a little tighter than you usually do.

IS IT JUST ME?

Malavika Sahoo

Do you also feel the ache?

Or is it just me?

The sudden pull that comes out of nowhere,

When I'm already in the future.

Everything aligns precisely with you and the way you said it all.

I find myself in the same position.

The same phase.

The same vibe.

The same fear.

The weather disagrees and resembles what my heart and soul wear.

The warmth vanishes, and arteries rupture.

The past presents itself again, slackening my grip on my emotions.

I can find myself in the same condition.

The same trace.

The same inscribe.

The same sphere.

Grey is all around, covering up what I had to share.

This is not what counts in my culture.

The adrenaline shoots up, and the dark darkens.

I can find my sentiments at the same auction.

The same pace.

The same dive.

The same lure.

Positioned in between my ignorance and my acceptance,

I had no notion about what to choose.

Choice being the cause of suffocation,

I would be suffering from asthma if I were to lose.

Do you also feel the ache?

Or is it just me?

LITTLE BERTHA

Simi Tiwari

Little Bertha saw blue,
When the skies woke up,
And the larks trilled down;
Another day of scrubbing shut windows.

Little Bertha saw yellow,
When the pail got tossed,
And drenched her about;
Another day of praise for a good doormat.

Little Bertha saw green,
When the grasslands swayed,
And shadows lurked in ridges;
Another day of Pied Piper's funny whims.

Little Bertha saw white,
When the dress is bunched up,
And her laces ripped off;
Another day of gathering shreds of self.

Little Bertha saw red,
When the fingers dug in,
And the skin lacerated;
Another day of screams no one heard.

Little Bertha saw black,
When the eyes just blinked,
And shoulders shrugged;
Another day of pretending it never happened.

BROKEN LOVE

Saisha Khemka

Feels like you're pushing me out of your life,
Every time I communicate with you.
Sometimes, I think you shout and shout.
Sometimes, I think that you don't care.
Sometimes, I feel broken inside.
Many times, I am sad and in despair,
I know that you love me,
But sometimes, you go too far.
Sometimes, you take me for granted,
And I feel so hurt inside.
And when I try to get close to you,
You sometimes push me away.

And each time you leave me for someone else,
I get this feeling of dismay.
I know you have many problems in life,
And I am here to help you through it all.
If you have some trust in me,
I'll be able to help you move on.

MICAWBER

Mahek Gupta

The world outside melts away, but I stay.
I lock the door and breathe in a quiet, calm sound.
Spinning webs layered with thoughts led astray.
In floating mid-existence, I unbound.

Escaping into myriad worlds, I pounce,
Upon each lone second abound and tie.
Bundles of spilling lives while I renounce,
Any connection to my earthly realm soul lies.

These fantasies serenade rot parts there.
A high spread through my stiff, unholy limbs,
Solidifies carving bones from drained air,
Materialising sucked atoms and wit.

Thus, I am made, perchance, a mere human,
Token crooked for a mad world, I lumen.

ALTER EGO

Bhakti Barad

I want to be seen;
I want to be heard;
I want to be well-read with books on my shelf.
I bought them when I was a teenager and never finished.
I want to file my grandparents' pictures to remember the day they fought on their way to their honeymoon.
I want to be dressed in chic and plaid skirts with my bare skin showing without the fear of strange hands.
I want to speak aloud and not just words but with angst,
My emotions slam the poetry I wrote.
I want to learn new words, words that I find magical, philosophical,
Historical words with power and voice,
I want to sink into the arms of that fictional boy,
Who I thought was real when I dreamt of him.
I want to find him, find him in someone.

I want to reach out to people's hands to save myself,
From falls rushing down my throat and up my neck.
I want to be intelligent, to speak for hours of paragraphs
to satisfy myself.
I want to learn physics and math and how the earth moves.
I want to watch classic movies to imagine myself,
In a new scenario, every day, to find an escape.
I want to be the male lead, to walk like an iron
and cry my eyes,
When I see my mum.
Hell, I want to be Forrest Gump.
I want to fit in, in the party of people where stories are made,
And destroyed, where love is found and lost,
Where hands are held at night beneath the blanket,
Fit into where glasses are poured over intellect,
And notice the world of dark academia and poetry,
Fit in my mother's jeans.

I want to love the freckle on his finger;
If he allows me, I want to be as pretty as a rose as in Titanic.
I want to be chosen, to be kept forever in a small,
fragile case of glass,
Somewhere like a rose in the museum of their eyes.
I want to be held tight, with everything he owns,
From palms, eyes, jackets and words.
I want to smell like a candle from the medieval times,
With lavender essence and innocence.
I want to be brave like the people battling puzzles in their
minds.

OFFENDER'S NEEDS

Pranjal Verma

You pick it up,
Give yourself a second to think,
And shower all your cruelty and brutality.
You tear my flesh off.
You leave your marks on me.
You offer me an unasked and unwanted present.
You punish me.
You push me down the stairs, pin me to the wall.
You let my head hurt and heart, which is the most important of all.
You let my fingers bleed, my flesh tear apart.
You lose yourself in your own world.
To me, you don't pay any heed.

Wondering if perhaps that's what an offender needs.
Offender of necessities, asking for too much.
Offenders of emotions, feeling too much.
Offender of the waters, letting the tears flow.
Offender of all the positive, perhaps feeling low.
The offender of your perception, offender of my own.
Offenders of this cruel world which is very well-known.
Wondering if perhaps that's what an offender needs.
To tear their flesh apart, to not be paid any heed.
To not look forward to.
To always feel lonely and lost.
To be always hurt at any cost.
Wondering if perhaps that's actually what an offender needs.
To be hurt and lost.
To be always broken at any cost.

WHILE IN PAIN

Keertika Shivee

Yes, I am in pain,
And no, it was not what I wanted to gain,
It was not something I would wish for anyone either,
It does not bring you hope, only darkness.
It does not make you feel good,
It does not make you feel wanted,
It makes you lost even when you have found it,
It makes you feel like a poet, writing your every emotion,
And when you have written everything,
Only then do you see that your words do not bring justice to your feelings,
It can make you see beauty in everything that goes around,
This made me wonder, was love what Shakespeare really found?

Pain does a funny thing to your soul every second it stays,

It keeps breaking you into pieces, promising to make you whole instead,

You might have read somewhere,

Pain demands to be felt;

So, you start to live in pain, thinking that now maybe it won't make your life hell,

But then people like me, you see, are born with this gift,

We make a home out of hurt, and we never leave.

The people whose souls are made of stardust and gold,

They live to be surrounded by darkness, maybe even get consumed whole,

So, pain does you more wrong than it does good,

It makes you believe that only being broken is for you,

It makes you smile even when the tears are true,

And you, my love,

You never understood.

SPACE POET'S HOPE

Bhakti Barad

My hopes fell in a pool of a dense night.
The subdued fear and intense shivers,
Take over my shoulders and tear it apart.
Clear pearls blanket my spine line,
The hopes swim and sink deeper.
Shade pokes out my iliac crest.
I never got the fern leaves tattoo,
The pain is just as much,
Austria will never be called the city of music,
With my screech in "The Cranberries,"
Today, it's the sixteenth trick or treat.
I've been tricked more often, bleached more often,
Then, the beach lingered on like a leech,
Wanting more of Sarah and Mitch.

What is Abercrombie and Fitch?
A space poet paints my paintings,
Mucked pastel across the collar,
As my bones pout inside a tin,
Teeth licking sourness in,
Feels more than normal,
Space poet stands by the door.
A boombox built-in,
My window pane shakes in the voice of "Musgraves."
It's too cute to take it to the grave,
My brutalized hopes decay,
In the space, the poet's boots.
I started walking barefoot,
Fly away in the galaxy dust,
With Sylvia Plath's bell jar,
Austria never seemed so far.

SUMMER FEASTS

Simi Tiwari

Third of May, you threw a feast,
With red ribbons and martinis.
Cheers to your profound speech,
And my eyes rimmed with pleas.

Satin dress down the stairs,
I raise my plastic smile.
Purple eyes from last night,
Head banged against the tile.

Curious hands to glittery gifts;
I slice my fingers through.
Paper cut for a paper anniversary,
Why was the blood blue?

Anaesthetic to frozen wounds,
You appear to numb the pain.
Alcohol doesn't heal injuries;
My cries go in vain.

Walls echo our fights and fall,
But love was in the air.
Tripping afresh on thin ice,
What I did was only fair.

I was your water lily once,
On rooftop bars and cab rides.
Watch me be a poison ivy;
Now that I buy you cyanides.

Third of June, I throw a feast,
With black ribbons and chamomile.
Sobs at my profound eulogy,
And your coffin in the aisle.

THAT NIGHT

Lokeshna Bulani

That night, your hands,
Didn't feel the shame.
When your eyes looked at me,
As it turned love into lust.
My hands became firm,
As I felt helpless,
Like a butterfly sensing danger.
I screamed with confusion,
As you tapped my mouth.
I felt pain as tears rolled over my cheek.
That night still haunts me.
Today, no touch feels safe on my skin.

THE DISTURBED STRING

Charvi Mishra

It was at this moment,
I felt like my life had taken a step back,
Instead of trying to climb the stairs again.
I simply stumbled down,
Even the last ounces of will be vanished into thin air.
Everything I aspired to be–was shattered.
I let go of the perceptions formed of me,
I let go of my ambitions and digressed away from my planned path.
I let go of myself.
Is it normal to lose all faith?

Because my mind's dried up as hope leaves my soul,

To lose conviction with every passing day,

Finally, the pot went empty today.

Disappointment dawns and swallows me more.

The crestfallen consumes me.

The paucity of self-love, logic, and reality make up this whirlpool.

Well, one remains unaware of the charms in life as much as the opposite of it.

The broken cube laid,

The scattered pieces expose the state of my mind.

THE GIRL IN PYJAMAS

Bhakti Barad

This is a story about a girl in pyjamas and a cranky little thing in her pool.

She is surrounded by the nauseous scent of alcohol-painted nails,

She curled up in a ball.

It's fall here in the mid-October,

Cheeks are dryer than all the maple leaves.

All her friends are lying on the grass with their hands,

In the backseat of the car, she sits in the middle,

Playing music for them feels just like a movie when they kiss in the end.

Girl in pyjamas is a wonderland in her own acts,

Mentally sitting with one numbed leg,

In a baseball shirt, screaming at her phone,

She can't escape this facade of a room.

Coincidentally, it's also painted blue.
Blue coffee mug sits idle like her,
She doesn't know all the pretty words,
All the cute boys or the cute girls.
She doesn't know how to feel love,
Only to feel the pain that goes above her throat.
Her fair skin, jealous all the time,
A girl that only bites,
A girl who laughs at her jokes,
A girl who chokes on her words,
A girl who is afraid of her world,
A girl in pyjamas is a messy girl,
An egocentric mind stalker,
Emotionless prick.
She plays all of her tricks,
Then, she shuts herself in a locker.
Calls herself an alien in a spaceship,
A girl so bad at relationships.
Is it a fault of her own that she's all alone?

WALKING FORTRESSES

Samriddhi Khawas

Wandering hands; innocent skin;
Promises without lust within.
A joke, a laugh;
A subtle sleight of hand,
And then the world turns black.
A muffled scream, a forceful hand,
The moon closes her eyes;
And unfolds a night of ineffable sins.
The mountains tremble with rage,
And all the stars wince.
Rhythmic movements, hollow screams,
White clothes torn at the seams;
A wooden floor slowly turning red;
Then one body runs away,
And the other drops down dead.
A new morning, the same old world
Sirens galore, the winds had spread the word;

'It is a plain story, really,' they say.
The body simply hit its head and died midplay.
A sunny day, a casket, a grave,
A hundred white roses, a lavish wake.
Tears and hugs and well wishes said,
A crowd unaware that the man who cried the loudest,
Had his sleeves painted red.
A year passes,
And another does, too;
The dead, so long gone.
But the grave remains barren,
Its epitaph is still new.
A world that walks on a blood-moistened earth.
A deaf and blind crowd;
Shrouded in pretence, or so goes the tale,
Where everyone has built a wall around themselves
So, all appear the same.
Walking fortresses tread the soft grass
And these walls around people,
These walls around hearts,
Render the power of the heavens inept,
To tell the victim and the villain apart!

REVENGE TAKEN

Pranjal Verma

There he stood with the weapon in his hands,
Ready to destroy me.
He was ready to fulfil his will, ready to seek revenge.
Revenge of fighting back in the dark,
With four men on the streets.
All alone, to accompany me was my spark.
Revenge for speaking too loud, wearing my choice,
With being shut up in a cage, not talking to boys,
With being forced and hit,
Being cut and split.
Revenge of inhaling some freshness.
Working in a cabin.
With all my books thrown in the garbage bin.
Revenge of being too silent.
Shutting up my mouth.
By listening to them and every insult they put out,

Revenge of fighting for me, standing out.
With being a spoiled brat in the house,
With being too outspoken and shouting too loud.
Revenge of keeping my emotions to myself,
Being able to not blurt everything out.
With getting quiet from always being ready to shout,
Revenge of being me, not killing my authenticity.
With now listening to them and enacting their way,
Now, opening my legs down, I lay.
The revenge was taken for everything I did.
Every time I did exist.
Every time I stood up.
Every time I got down.
The weapon scraped my flesh from certainly every single side,
As I was forced to open myself wide.
With four of them getting one by one aside,
After they worse-ship my intimacy,
With me doing all that I could hide.
The revenge was taken well to teach me a lesson.
That a girl like me here isn't meant to reside,
Because I was too outspoken and wild.

US

Shari Gharat

We were deranged,

Like two boxers throwing endless punches,

Till one of their jaws breaks.

We killed each other with words and breathed back life with kisses.

We drank too much, we drank too little,

We hit each other, and we iced the wounds afterwards,

But burned flowers don't bring back life with them,

And then we were lost.

Lives were threatened,

But favourite songs were sung right after.

Minds were torn apart,

But torsos intertwined with one another.

Forest fires from the cigarettes that we smoked began right in the centre;

And spread everywhere,
Burning all near and distant.
You said you loved the tides,
How the sun and the moon guided the ocean,
How the waves hit the shore,
The water blue and warm and cool,
But maybe you forgot they also went in, all the way in,
To the deep and distant land,
Tearing everything in two along the way.
All that, and yet I remember loving you.
Growing old with you.
But the tides came and ruined it once again.

STRANGERS

P. Navya

It was an unexpected moment when we met.
Yes, we carried a flawless relationship full of joy.
What no one could ever envision, including us.
But later, I noticed,
It was only a one-sided affection.
Still, I kept up hope in our friendship.
Unfortunately, you ruined it with your actions.
You wanted to mend it.
But now I knew it.
There is no point in anything.
I wanted to know.
Do I really matter to you?
If yes, then why did I see you walking in different directions?

Leaving me in the middle of the ocean.
Is that really what I mean to you?
It is almost crushing.
But I gained all the strength to say 'no.'
Because I don't want to get hurt again.
There is nothing I can try to reunite us.
It is always me who makes the first move.
So, I am done now, as you have proven.
You don't need me anymore.
Just as with all other broken glasses,
You are no different than those broken glasses.
Only the way it happened.
One day, I'll burn each and every memory of yours.
No matter how hard it is for me.
Anyway, I didn't lose a friend.
I have discerned I never had one.

THE WAY THEY CEASE

Pranjal Verma

You flash at my eyes, blocking my vision.
Your hand goes around in search of its destination.
They cease and let me sense all the pain I ever felt.
They cease and leave their unerasable impressions in the form of scars.
They cease and scrape off all the flesh my body had.
They cease and pull them apart with all the energy they had
They cease and hurt me, and again they rewind
They cease and drag me by my hair,
And throw me off to the side.
Then, they cease and pull another girl,
And yank her off the serenity in which she did reside.
They cease and tear every girl apart from each and every side.

They cease and cause destruction of the peace and
calm one holds inside.

They cease and cause hurt and tears.

Give a reason to drown in melancholy.

Then they finally continue to go around after getting
all the need,

But they do not rest; they cease.

TO-DO LIST FOR THE DAY

Kanak Modi

Colours do not hold significance as my feelings always scream.

People's individuality is like dark and blue,

Only to turn my feelings to uneasiness to wreak me during my midnight grief.

I indulge in pottery to shape my rage into vessels.

However, I fail to express my feelings in those lifeless clay symbols.

I weave my grief into garments,

Only to stare at them when I get a moment's break.

My entire life feels like a big mistake,

Only to drink Vodka for my feelings' sake.

WHEN IT'S NEAR

Callum Wilson

When it's nearby,
I can feel like I'm in a world of pure imagination.
Let it be,
Watch me go, my lovely fellows.
Now it's here.
And, I can't bear to even keep my eyes up.
Faces merge into the mud,
A thick grime of sweaty puddle paranoia.
And now I'm there with the stares,
And the ringing doesn't stop to hold me.
Oh, it falls down, it pours,
Like a river of coaxing silence.
Oh, it flows gently into the cold of panic.

So don't tell me,
Don't let me,
Don't touch,
And let me sit down.
I've been so tired,
Too tired to sleep,
Break down to begin,
Waking, gentle jelly moments.
I stood there on the train.
I thought that I shouldn't really be thinking.
Faint purple light leaks,
And mixes with the blurry mass to dull me.
The time to prepare was before.
My knuckles were white,
But I kept them on the rail because everything else was a heady,
A slurry of concentrated aggravation.
The conductor raised the tumult into a frenzy of squealing recorders,

And tremulous contrabass saxophones and undulating
wheezing, accordions and brazen harmonica madness,
and then,

The choir joined in howling amidst mechanical prostration
and vehement absurdity in their stupid, uninformed
acquiescence screaming bloody murder on the train.

The platform embraced me like a bullet into concrete.

I closed my ears and cried because there was nothing else,
I could do.

It was just too loud on the train.

That was all.

YOU'RE STUCK

Kanak Modi

You show up in a new crisp suit and laugh,

With fifty-some people gazing at you, you are from a shady corner.

You're stuck.

I see you gulp alcohol like you'd drown someone.

They think you're fun.

You smash things under the sun and gaze at my lips in the dark.

You're stuck, and I ask you for help.

You overflow with rage and beat me instead.

The following morning, you grin like it's a pathetic joke that would make my cheeks red.

I respect the intent and slap you.

You grin harder.

I give up.

I leave for work before you finish your toast.

Then I sprint across the sidewalk out my gate before you can keep tabs on me.

Why do you keep tabs on me?

I don't ask you.

I'm not scared.

I'm not scared.

You told me you'd love me forever.

I've been waiting for four years.

My friends giggle and say they'd help me.

I sigh in relief and drive back home.

It's funny.

Come on, it is a little funny.

Isn't it?

You're stuck but wouldn't ask for help.

EVE

Tarini Bhatia

Introduction

Eve, sixteen, was born on a sacred Tuesday morning
in January.

She is sure she gets her anger from her father,

But she's more afraid of her rage than anyone else.

Major Events

At eight, she realised that food tasted better when
you had someone to share it with.

She stopped eating when she was alone, so during recess, she
walked around her school building because she couldn't eat.

At nine, she made her sister cry and told her she loves her,

She still hasn't been able to say it, maybe because that's how
it has always been.

At ten, she wanted to tell her father good night but stood in front of his room for fifteen minutes before giving up.

At eleven, she made coffee for the first time, and her father loved it; he still asks her to make it occasionally, equivalent to them saying I love you.

That is all she will get, and it's okay if there's room for coffee.

At thirteen, she noticed the lull that comes after every earthquake and that the aftershock,

is never too far away,

Sometimes, that is alright when people love you.

At fourteen, she perceived the world as a better place when she was eating alone, so she stopped eating around the people who loved her,

Which is to say that she was never eating, and it was okay because people finally loved her.

At fifteen, she realised that nothing about that Tuesday morning was sacred and that it was another mundane day because no matter how many times she turned to God,

He turned her away.

She knew she was a child of destruction and nothingness,

Sprung out of black holes and triangles that held everything, yet nothing.

At sixteen, she was told that her anger came from her ancestors and wondered if they feared themselves, too.

Why does it seem like she could swallow the universe whole if not?

Interview

When asked to describe herself, she said she was kind but not too kind.

She continued about how her sister was too kind and wished she could tell her that.

When asked about her fears, she said that sometimes she fears she isn't kind and will always be twelve years old and lonely.

She likes watching Bojack Horseman and Grey's Anatomy, Fleabag, and all kinds of comedy shows.

She thinks her best feature is her smile because people have said so.

She loves frogs and all the shades of the colour blue.

ON BEING THE CHILD OF DESTRCUTION

Tarini Bhatia

The universe sighs when it holds me in its arms and looks for places to hide me because I'm the child of destruction, and every breath that I take is capable of shaking the galaxies,

even the ones that are far away.

The Milky Way trembles by my name, the stars flicker and lose their light, and the sun stands still despite all his might because I exist.

The rivers change their direction when they see my rage,

The blooming flowers die, and the earth wants to split open and hide me somewhere because the universe trembles when I exist.

This is my father's anger, and I have nothing to do with it, except when I spill some coffee over my assignment, or I forget to tie my hair on a windy day, or when I look in the mirror and hate what I see or when I love someone so much that I can barely breathe.

Then, the anger is mine. I own it. I have nurtured it.

The way it burns my skin when I feel the rage running through my veins,

I've given it nourishment.

It burns because I provide it with fuel.

It burns because I exist.

My mother taught me to breathe in, but she got to teach me how to breathe out, and now I'm stuck with my tongue in between my teeth.

No words come out of my mouth, so instead, I sit alone and do quizzes on YouTube.

I don't know much about myself except that if I were a colour,

I would be blue, and if I were a season,

I would be monsoon.

If I were a drink,

I would be black coffee, and if I were a type of plant,

I would be one of those evergreen ones,

Which is weird because evergreen plants don't shed their leaves,

But I can bet I have been losing parts of myself since I was born.

Autumn was never here, but I was.

I have lost because I exist.

I look at my reflection, and I see someone who isn't me, and when I ask them who they are, they tell me that they are destruction.

They are using my body as a shelter, and they are not a part of me, but it would've been better if they were because something that was a part of me would have been kinder to me instead when I looked in the mirror and screamed.

All I can hear are muffled sounds of laughter and destruction, telling me that I am in pain because I exist.

SHORT STORIES

ONE

A PATHWAY OF NIGHTMARES

Tulsi Nambiar

Nightmares strangled her in the night. Memories barricaded her way during the day. She slept with regret and woke up in pain. This is what loss does to you. Her husband was confined to a hospital bed, and he screamed and shouted out for her to help, but she could not; she was more helpless than he was. She hid her helplessness, and instead, she tried to soothe him. She patted his shoulder and held his hand as he endured pain and suffocation within his body. He shouted louder and louder; it was no longer controllable; she fought hard to keep her tears jailed as she saw him suffer. He twisted and turned as the medications spread across his blood. He shivered, and she held on to him to keep him steady or herself; she knew not. Nothing helped; his shouts became monotonous and routine, and even his screams had gotten used to the pain.

*****

Breathless, she woke up. She sat up, her hands on either side behind her; she looked up at the ceiling almost as if it was watching her. Shoba got up and quickly gulped down water from the kitchen. This had become her new routine; nearly every other night, she would find herself having the same nightmare.

There was not much she could do to avoid having the nightmare. Shoba went to a therapist, hoping to find some solace. The therapist listened to her cry and described her loss. None of which put a stop to her nightmares. Her therapist told her to join a group, you know, the ones people with addiction often go to; they sit in large circles and talk about their life, and the others are forced to listen and applaud you for telling your story. She hated those but tried. She could not relate to or see herself as one of the stories. Later on, her therapist suggested that talking to someone who shared the same grief and loss could help. She called her children and tried to speak to them. However, it was of no help. She could not articulate the words when she talked to her son; he was too busy.

On the other hand, her daughter had blocked her mind from the loss and focused on her small family instead. The last thing the therapist suggested was to go on a trip. She went on a cruise with her college friends for five days. It was fun and enjoyable, but every night, the nightmares remained.

*****

Shoba gave up on the therapist and focused on looking after her mother. It did not help with the nightmares, but during the day, she was not lonely. She cooked, cleaned, and conversed with her mother for the first few months, but soon, conversation became rare, and loneliness returned.

There was no one to argue with or tell her that there was no salt in her curry. No one told her to make sweets, and there was no one to say to her. Sometimes, she would find herself sitting in her bedroom, knees tucked to her chest, staring blankly at a house so empty. She wished he was sitting on the other side telling her how mischievous he was as a child, but instead, there was only a crumpled white bedsheet on which she slowly fell asleep.

He could not move and kept shouting. He was intertwined in IV tubes; high-concentration drugs flowed through them and intoxicated his body. The tubes choked his neck and twisted around his bony wrists. It seemed like the tubes were slithering across his body like snakes.

She aimlessly tugged at the tubes, hoping to free him. It was a futile action, but she kept tugging. Her hands ached, and he was still trapped. She pulled harder and harder.

She woke up and found the bedsheet circled and twisted around her. Her breathing was rapid, and she realised it was the first time she had physically responded to her nightmares. She did not have enough time with a nightmare to get used to it, and they played in her mind throughout the day.

*****

The bell rang, and she went to get the door; the mailman had three envelopes addressed to her late husband. She took them in her hands and, one by one, opened them, hoping that her husband would magically appear near her. The envelopes did no such thing; they screamed out numbers that had to be paid, all with the money he had left her. From apartment maintenance to electricity bills, they all had to be paid.

These were times when she realised how dependent she was on her husband. These were times when she resented him because he never taught her these things. He never told her about the bills. She was left to figure it out independently and decided to do so the next day. One might think resentment towards a person makes the loss less painful, but it does not. Did it make it worse? Perhaps. Did it continue? Always.

As night approached, she prayed, hoping to sleep peacefully. The doors shut, and the walls closed in on her. The walls were painted with numbers similar to bills. Shoba held her husband's wallet and stared helplessly at the walls. They continued to come closer to her. She opened the wallet, and instead of money, she found photos of their wedding day, family vacations, and their precious moments together. She was suffocating with memories in hand and reality around her.

*****

She woke up. Yet another nightmare. Each month, a new nightmare would play in her mind, and each time, her mind would go back to the same day. The body was brought into their ancestral home. Shoba sat in a corner, leaning her head on the wall. She watched her late husband. The pain was excruciating inside her head. But she did not cry. People rushed in and out, offered their condolences, drank a cup of tea, and left. Eventually, the bustling house became silent as the funeral rituals began. Shoba still sat in the corner with a blank expression. After the rituals, the body was lifted to be carried out, and his face would no longer be seen.

Tears rolled down. She wailed. Her sobs echoed in the ginormous house. No one could offer her any consolation. Her pain and loss were immeasurable. It was beyond limits. She felt truly alone.

Slowly, she gathered her thoughts, came back to the present, and came to terms with the fact that she could never truly accept her husband's death. She would always feel alone, and she would always have those nightmares. It was agonising, but there it was, that's what loss does to you, and she welcomed yet another night of nightmares.

TWO

THE HEART BREAK OF A TRAGIC HERO

Anirban Dutta

The feelings of deep pain are hard to fade, it remains in the background for time immemorial. The day began with the unending autumn thunderstorms with a sudden gentle blow of the wet soil mixed and matched with the long-lost nostalgia of a past that shines brightly. Such is the case of a young, nostalgic writer interested in exploring the hues and beauty that stands against the cramped, old world. As the weather starts to go wild, the writer wakes up in a room filled with the odour of unpublished notes that accumulated dust with the fast-paced time that waits for no one. The writer began his day in his notepad with pages filled with extended lengths of paragraphs that no one accepts. He gets up and sits in the rocking chair as the rain stops, undeterred by the outside world.

*****

He suddenly journeys to his rooftop as he sits at the shed. The time races by as water accumulates on his roof. The writer, lost in his own thought, plays out the episodes in his life where rejections became his constant company. A company which is bleeding his life out to soak his future in a grilling machine that accepts each piece to be similar. The writer pays attention to his notepad making notes where he sees numerous scratches claiming to give voice to his work as it is deprived of the courage to be known to the outside world. He sits outside his modest lodgings to set out in the world, only to hear another rejection of his work.

*****

He dreams of committing suicide only to gleam life, leaving his lifeless body. As he heads back to the main street, he sees himself amidst numerous homeless people whose cries get lost in everyone's ears. He feels shattered, deceived by the world that feasts on the creative minds destined to meet heartbreak at the end as the life of a tragic young writer break piece by piece like a broken mirror, never to become whole. Many of his write-ups end in the editor's trash, leaving him with no choice but to stare at the river where the "dinghy" (boat) fades with the cloud in the distance as his dream of being a writer slips away once again. The young writer's life passes from days to months with no success, making him a tragic hero in his own story, where the main character looks deceased with heartbreak as torn pieces of his draft blow in the wind of the editor's gloomy office.

The heartbreak of a tragic hero makes his life inanimate as tears dry up with his monetary struggles to live in a society that denies creativity. His heavy heart with his shaky hands makes him scribble the pages once more as the genre turns from romantic poems to the daily struggle of his life. Each second sounded like years to him as his wall clock continued to tick in a room with a candle and a shadow that raced non-stop. The face of the shadow reveals a writer slowly returning to his curiosity with a creative mind that nurtures a different universe away from his surroundings and reality. The scribbled pages turn up in the hands of another publisher the next day, making the writer turn his back once more with the submitted piece.

*****

The day started with rains taking their break as the sky cleared up for the sun to arrive. The writer's day, like any day, started with his notepad as his age-old, semi-charged device beeped with a call. The face of the young writer gleamed as he saw queues of readers standing with a book in his name. He saw the years of struggle, baggage getting down with the stroke of pen running deep into the page, making the minute ink dots settle around his name in the author's column. The unfulfilled writer with no voice suddenly felt tears as years of heavy baggage suddenly seemed less with his spectacled face getting new curves of experience.

THREE

A CONVERSATION WITH HER

Nainika Chaudhari

'You're not me.'

She isn't. She's different in all the subtle ways. She's wrong; a mistake needs to be hidden. To be perfected before anyone sees her.

'I am.'

She can't be. I'll no longer be able to live in denial, to look at her and see what everyone else sees.

I asked, 'Why do you look like that?'

'It's how we've always been. Why do you not like us? We've supported you, helped you, been there for you.'

The hour hand showed three. The minutes ticked by; each one turned out like a roar in the quiet hall.

*****

'I've only ever known to hate you,' My confession was whispered. I had already given up.

'Were you taught to only look at the bad things?'

'I don't do that.'

It was a lie.

'Of-course you don't.'

She knew that, too.

'I can't just focus on the assets; how will I improve?'

'But you don't. You don't improve. You just sit in front of me for hours, doing nothing but criticising.'

When did I start? When did I fall into this hole? When do I stop?

'Did you never realise the light in our eyes dimming after every hurtful word? Did you just stop caring? Are you doing this purposefully, trying to become a shell of a person?'

'No.'

'We were beautiful. We laughed, we danced, we sang poetry to ourselves. Why did you stop?'

She didn't understand.

'What do I not understand? I sit here, helpless on the other side, and see you create scars with your words. I see you looking at me with hate; every burning look, a knife to my heart. It's only you who I have to rely on to pick me up; I only have us and no one else. How do you expect me to love the person who hates me the most?'

*****

The glass shatters. Shards stick to a fist, blood slowly dripping down. I looked back at her. She's smiling now, head tilted to the side, every part of her multiplied in the cracks. Her soft stomach sticking out, her shoulders high.

'I am you. I'm the part of you desperate for your acceptance and affection. Don't make me beg for it. Don't starve me for you to look a different way; don't hit me when you mess up. It's me who's going to be with you until death and forever after; treat me with the same understanding you give everyone else.'

'Please.'

I let the tears roll down.

FOUR

A LETTER FROM ME

Tulsi Nambiar

Dear young girl,

I was back on the battleground. My enemy stood before me; the repulsive figure was back to haunt me. I was all alone with my rival; I had ample time to examine her weaknesses, flaws, wrongdoing, scars, and unnatural features. The antagonist in my life had made me suffer from insomnia during the nights and act as a hurdle whenever I decided to do something. You must wonder who is this vile and cruel foe of mine, my body.

She was a dangerous enemy. She made me see things I had never imagined before. She made me feel worse than I had ever felt before. There were times when she made me denigrate everything I saw. She made my eyes too sharp, and she made my smile disappear.

She knew how to creep into my thoughts, and she did so with the stealth of a snake. There were times when I would be reading a book all curled up, and she would remind me of her existence, make me aware of the fat I could feel around me, and question my shape. Immediately, I would leave everything and run to the mirror. I stood in front of the mirror and looked deep into it with defeat in my eyes; she had won again and successfully disrupted my peace.

My enemy was so hungry, and this hunger was never satisfied. Her hunger was eating me away, reaching the bottom of an innocent soul.

You must think, 'Oh, how silly a girl she is, she should just get over it.' That is precisely what I told myself, except my enemy's words, 'You are hideous to look at,' were more effective.

In the nights, as I lay in bed, she would knock a thought into my mind, 'You forgot the mirror today.' It was a simple line; it was not a command, a question, or a plain statement but a fact. But I saw it as a command. On a chilly night, I effortlessly undressed, went to the mirror, and turned on the brightest light in the room.

First, I stood, the right side of my body being the first casualty of the night. I inspected my face; to begin with, a pimple was all I saw. I moved down to my chest; something looked wrong, I thought. I looked down further to my torso, which was meant to be flat, and I saw a bump instead. She, my superior rival, forced my eyes to look at my legs, and there I saw it. A small tributary of white blemishes that had no proper beginning or end. I touched them, and they were etched onto my skin. I felt one tear run down my face.

I turned to face the mirror directly. It was no longer one tear that tumbled down my cheeks. The body shape in the mirror was far from perfect; there were curves in all the wrong places, and the white scars were more visible. My stretch marks stretched across from my waist down to my thighs, and there were scars on my knees.

I turned so my left side became the next chosen casualty, and my blurry eyes scanned the view in the mirror. She showed my eyes the stretch marks that flowed from my waist down on this side of my body. The marks on my body looked like a deformed tarantula trying to capture every part of my body. It made me twitch with hatred, and I found myself pursing my lips together, and the sobs were left to echo in my bowels.

Everything I saw that night made me self-conscious; they made my intestines twist and sicken. I despised the image I saw, which was imperfect beyond measure.

Disgust, rage, guilt, and sadness overtook me as I went back to bed.

I was disgusted because of my body's ugliness.

I was angry because I felt helpless.

I was guilty because I had let my body reach such a stage.

I was sad because I hated my body.

In bed, I wondered how I would never look attractive in certain clothes. They asked how I would never find a partner who found me attractive. I wondered how my friends might leave me if they saw me underneath my clothes. It walked to how my existence might abash my own family.

I believed that my body was my identity and nothing else mattered. My body was the only thing people focused on. Was I wrong? Was I wrong to believe the things I did?

*****

I was on my way to shower. However, the mirror stopped me. I was aware of my enemy yet again. I lifted my arm and saw white stripes slashed across most of my arm; their existence crept up overnight. A tear rolled down my cheek. I was panic-stricken and pulled out my phone. I flooded Google with questions.

Can you get rid of stretch marks?

Are stretch marks permanent?

Why do stretch marks appear?

But I wanted to ask whether they lessen my value in the world of perfect bodies.

In my eyes, they did—a body with callous skin and discoloured marks all over. In a world where everyone was attaining the perfect body shape, I felt alone as I had nothing close to it. There was no value for mine. My body demeaned who I was in the world.

At that moment, when I realised that I had an undesirable body, I wanted to rip my skin apart. I dug my nails into my skin and dragged it along wherever I could, and I wanted to see my skin disappear. I wanted to see those white stripes disappear. But all my nails did was cause red lines that made my skin more noticeable.

Tears flooded my face. They represented my defeat. I had given in to my enemy without a fight. I started feeling every part of my body from then on. When I walked, and my arm touched my torso, she immediately reminded me of the stretch marks there. If my thighs stuck to each other on a hot day, she made me feel the stretch marks, and my smile would dissolve.

I stopped wearing most of my clothes. I shifted to wearing clothes that were baggy and hung loosely on me. Even when I could feel the clothes on my skin, my heartbeat would rise, and I would undress in front of a mirror in no time.

Crowded places made me anxious. I felt how a lone baby

without its mother would think on a bustling road, vulnerable, cranky, and paranoid. I could feel too much of my skin, and the urge to run to the mirror was almost irresistible. I felt everyone's eyes on me, almost like they could see all my flaws, and I had nowhere to hide. My foe suffocated me with my skin vigorously; I had no room to escape. In crowded rooms, all I could see were slim women; if they were not, at least they had smooth skin like butter. And the hold my enemy had around my neck would tighten so much so that I wanted to run away into the wilderness where none of it mattered.

One week passed, and after another week, she showed me a new flaw every week. Sometimes, it was an extra stream that was to become part of the tributary of stretch marks. Sometimes, it was some excess fat that had accumulated around my stomach or between my thighs. Other times, they were just reminders of flaws I knew existed.

Now and then, when I started to feel better and accept my body, she would say, 'The mirror is close by.' I always obeyed and walked to the mirror like a programmed robot, and when I saw the image, all of my insecurities returned without hesitation. I crouched in the corner of the room and let the tears fall.

I heard a voice. 'What is happening? What are you doing? Why are you naked? Why are you crying?'

I looked up at my mother. I wanted to tell her. I wanted to say I need help. I hate my body. I hate everything about myself. I am insecure. I'm not like the rest of them. But I knew my mother would tell me to breathe, and she would tell me it was only inside my head.

I pleaded with her, my enemy, let me speak up, get better, help me. But the only words that came out of my mouth were 'I can't,' and I continued to sob as my mother fetched my clothes for me.

She held me as I cried. I wailed out loud. I screamed. I sobbed. My lips trembled. My body shook with sorrow. I could not stop. I knew I was a disappointment to my mother, but my tears continued to soak her clothes.

Everything I felt, pain, sadness, guilt, anger, and disappointment, all these nights, they were silent; they knew no sound. But today, they found their voice in the form of my sobs. I wish I could do better. I hope I can get better. But all I could do was expect.

You must give a voice to your emotions. Maybe you should not let the white blemishes of your skin dictate your feelings. Perhaps you should not see your body as your enemy. But how can you not? I wish I knew the answers.

If only my body did not exist.

With pain,
Another girl

FIVE

DYING HOPE

Aryan Malkani

I had been living in a state of nightmare for years, only to dream that someday I would wake up to someone I can share emotions with. The friends who took everything away from me gave back nothing but a slap to my face with the gradually developing reality, which is dark, harsh and uncanny. The pain of giving my heart and soul to a person and getting nothing in return took away the one thing that kept me going – hope. The hope of life returning to normal, having a true permanent friend, and being confident about myself again was gradually fading.

*****

The news of school reopening became a nightmare, with no lights entering my blacked-out mind. However, a sense of optimism suddenly crossed my mind, but a serene, upbeat person in my soul was long dead. I entered the school building with a heavy heart. A sudden rush of adrenaline with the initiation of regular classes made me wipe off my sweat. I joined the class with a sudden beating in my heart.

A massive sigh of relief emerged in my mind when my eyes stared at the empty benches and chairs. I sat down with shaking legs and fingers while waiting for someone to come. However, I was still terrified. I left my seat and went near the window, biting my nails in anticipation. I gazed out the window to see some old friends and familiar faces on their way to school from the closed doors and windows of the confined classroom. The classroom suddenly changed with the hustle and bustle of smiles and laughter. The cold breeze and the lyrics of Billie Eilish's "Come Out and Play" started to get in every corner of the lifeless classroom.

Finally, the class door opened. The butterflies in my stomach turned into pterodactyls, my face pale. Joy and laughter filled the room while fear and anxiety crowded my head. The smile on my face went pale as I saw the classroom door opening. I was not afraid anymore, but the child in me had never changed with time. Time and tide have promised to keep my hopes alive, and I am attempting to do my best. Suddenly, the lunch break bell rang, and everyone left to meet their friends.

I tried looking for anyone not talking but remained silent with my head down. The thought of self-doubt triggered me to keep myself from crying. I roamed across the corridor on my own. The lively corridor failed to nurture life in me. A friendless existence embodied by waves of fear could not pierce my heart with the bright sunshine of the setting sun.

A realisation struck me like lightning. The sunshine I had dreamt of in the cage for two years was a cold, heavy downpour. Everything broke down. Surrounded by a dark aura, I stumbled to the bathroom. I locked myself in, leaning against the door, hugging my knees, and staring at the consequences of my failed attempts at bravery.

All hope was dead again.

SIX

ALL HE HAD, WAS SOME QUERIES

Ankur Mondal

On a fatal summer night, every floor of the house, bolting them inside, was under the comfort of their ceiling fans and water coolers. Television was at its highest decibel, competing and trying to suppress the neighbour's cacophony.

Between all these, Aarav was trying to complete his homework. Playful, kind-hearted, cultured, sweet, cute, pure at its own kind, intelligent, bright—these are a few synonyms that could describe him. Aarav, in his middle school, was a bit different than the regular kids. A soft-spoken child who was nurtured very delicately by his relocated parents. Elder sibling to his loving sister. Even a tiny argument could get him into pain and make him cry. He excelled in co-curricular activities as a painter, the choir's lead singer, and an impassioned dancer. Sports were never his forte. When all the kids spent time on the field tossing the ball, he spent it under the tree, in the corner of the shadowed pillar, or in the music or art room. He was often mocked, too. But with time, he mastered the art of evading.

*****

Everything was fine except his fear of a few subjects, which is again common to any ordinary kid. Everyone surely can't excel in everything. His family couldn't afford private home tuition. So, he often used to land up in Mr. Mukherjee's room.

Mr. Raja Mukherjee, a well-built, handsome finance professional and bachelor in his mid-20s, used to live in one of the small quarter rooms on the terrace of the same house. Being a person of the same community, he was regular and had a hold on Aarav's home, too. He liked reading Hindi murder mysteries and detective novels.

Like other days, Aarav showed up with his science book. All he again had was some queries. Raja, lying in the middle of the floor over his belly, bare-chested with a torn pair of pyjamas sliding down his torso, was reading another novel. The room, consisting of a foldable bed, a cooler, an earthen water pot, and a few pieces of luggage containing his daily wear, was tiny and quite empty. Aarav was called in and was asked to bolt the door to keep the room cool. He was instructed to read a chapter while Raja completed his. Later, he sat down and explained to Aarav his queries.

It was like a regular flow until his hand slid into Aarav's shorts. Unknowing of things and Raja's spontaneity, Aarav was numb. Till he could understand anything, Raja had his Mickey. He touched, mouthed, and jacked him off. His numbness was overpowered by a sense of relief, confusion, and disgust. This time, he couldn't even shed a tear, as he couldn't understand anything. All his eyes could see was Raja's horrified smile, a finger on his lips, and the other hand cleaning Aarav's fluids in his pyjamas. Aarav was summoned not to talk about this incident to anyone, as his parents would not believe him, and he would again become a subject of mockery. Raja knew his weakness really well. He took him to the restroom to get him cleaned and took off his clothes, too, and this time Raja jacked in front of him. He watched it all, standing helpless. And that was his first physical encounter with abuse.

*****

With the passing days, Aarav grew comfortable with his own abuser. The intimacy mushroomed between them. From shower to bed, Raja was teaching him a lot, which was inappropriate for his age. Lust homicides the kid's innocence. Aarav's life was no longer normal. He thrived on this strange feeling called love. After getting back from school, he used to yearn for his sight. Running up the stairs and escorting him to his door, he did it all.

This lasted placidly for almost thirty-six months till Raja decided to tie the knot with a lady his mother chose for him. Aarav could see that his time was getting divided and neglected like zilch. And with time, it became dreadful till Raja left that noon when Aarav was in his school. He cried all that night, hiding his tears from all. The abuse that the child mistook for love has left a lasting impact on his mental health and broken him forever.

The playful, kind-hearted, cultured, sweet, cute, and bright boy was nowhere to be found. He was cursing himself in his own grievance. All he wished was, 'Had he not had a query that night?'

CONTRIBUTING AUTHORS

CALLUM WILSON is from New Castle, United Kingdom. Callum is a lover of literature and poetry. He is the author of two poems, "Head Pipes" and "Train of Thought."

SIMI TIWARI is settled in York, United Kingdom. She is a student of Film & Literature at the University of York. As a literature student, she loves reading classic novels, watching films and writing. Simi has authored two poems, "Little Bertha" and "Summer Feasts" in the anthology.

MAHEK GUPTA is settled in Chicago, United States. She is an Editor for Seaglass Literary and a staff writer for Firefly Archives, Jamais Vu Zine. Mahek started writing poems when she was eight and has not stopped writing since then. Mahek has three poems in the anthology.

TARINI BHATIA is a student of Psychology at the University of Delhi. She loves poetry, writing, drawing, art and aesthetics. She is the author of two poems titled, "On Being the Child of Destruction" and "Eve."

SAKHI SINGH has completed her graduation from Miranda House, University of Delhi. She has published her book, "Affected Admiration." She has authored a poem titled "Growing Up" in the anthology.

SHRISTHI TIBDEWAL is a content writer with an interest in storytelling. She is a lover of arts, aesthetics, poetry and literature. Shristhi has authored a poem titled "The Nomad" in the anthology.

NAINIKA CHAUDHARI is a writer and has been published in various literary journals. She is the author of a short story titled "A Conversation With Her."

CHARVI MISHRA is from Mumbai. She is a student of Cognitive Science. Charvi is interested in writing, music and community development activities. She has authored a poem titled "The Disturbed String."

PRANJAL VERMA is an author and poet. She is a lover of poetry. Pranjal has authored two books.

SAISHA KHEMKA is a lover of poetry and songs. She is the author of a poem titled "Broken Love." Saisha likes to express her feelings and thoughts with a twist of poetry and music.

BHAKTI BARAD is a Psychology major. Bhakti likes watching documentaries with a focus on crime. She is also a fan of literature and art. Bhakti likes writing, and she has authored three poems in the anthology.

ARYAN MALKANI is a lover of literature and poetry. He is enthusiastic about music and art. He is the author of a short story titled "Dying Hope."

MALAVIKA SAHOO is a student. She is an admirer of arts, literature and photography. Malavika is the author of a poem titled "Is it just me?"

ANKUR MONDAL is an ad-film producer. He has co-authored four books and is a strong advocate of LGBTQ+ rights. Ankur loves to travel with his partner to untapped destinations to explore humanity and diversity and capture through his video travelogues. He is also a lover and an admirer of photography, singing and writing. Ankur has authored "Dwindling" and "All He Had, Was Some Queries."

TULSI NAMBIAR is a book lover and voracious reader. She loves writing and literature. She has authored two short stories, "A Letter From Me" and "A Pathway of Nightmares."

SHRAVANI KAPOOR is a student at Chatrabhuj Narsee School. She is interested in photography and literature and has a knack for writing. Shravani has authored two poems, "Perfect" and "Dark Minds."

LOKESHNA BULANI is from Agra, India. She is a student and is an aspiring poet and writer. She has authored multiple pieces for her school magazine since she was nine. Her passion for writing has enabled her to search for ideas. Lokeshna has written a poem titled "That Night" as a part of the anthology.

SHARI GHARAT is a girl from a small town and is now in love with a huge city. She loves to read and write. She wants to express herself using poetry. She is the author of a poem titled "Us."

P. NAVYA is based in Hyderabad. She is working as a Website Analyst and is a full-time Architect. She has completed her Architecture & Interior Design degree from the Jawaharlal Nehru Architecture and Fine Arts University. Navya has also completed her Master's in Business Administration (MBA) in Marketing. She has also contributed a poem titled "Strangers."

SAMRIDDHI KHAWAS is a student of Economics from the University of Calcutta. Apart from her passion in her subject of expertise, she is also interested in poetry and literature. Samriddhi is a voracious reader of poems. Her dream is to become an Economist. Samriddhi has authored a poem titled "Walking Fortresses" as a part of the anthology.

KEERTIKA SHIVEE is a lover of poetry and literature. She is the author of a poem, "While in pain."

ACKNOWLEDGEMENTS

The success process for every book is a direct result of the collaborative effort. "Cold Ashes" is no exception. I extend my sincere gratitude and thanks to the people involved in ensuring the anthology's success. Thanks to Anush Goel, the Founder of Inkfeathers, who extended his unique ideas and thoughts to the anthology. I sincerely thank the Marketing Manager, Yashika, who played a critical role in support related to the social media marketing strategies. I extend my thanks to all the authors who have provided their sincere assistance and made contributions to the anthology wholeheartedly. I would also like to extend my special thanks to my parents, who provided me moral support and courage to complete the anthology. My sincere appreciation goes to my late maternal grandpa, Prof. (Dr) Paritosh Sanyal, whose literary works inspired me to make this book a reality.

www.ingramcontent.com/pod-product-compliance
Lightning Source LLC
LaVergne TN
LVHW090052160826
845672LV00015B/1645

* 9 7 8 8 1 1 9 4 8 3 4 2 6 *